WHAT'S THE MOST BEAUTIFUL THING YOU KNOW ABOUT HORSES?

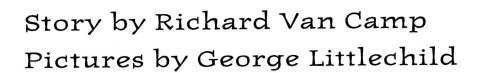

Story by Richard Van Camp
Pictures by George Littlechild

CHILDREN'S BOOK PRESS • SAN FRANCISCO, CALIFORNIA

Today it is forty below

in my hometown of Fort Smith
in the Northwest Territories of Canada.
It is winter and I am cold.
Not even my long johns and parka
can help me today.

It is so cold the ravens refuse to fly.
My dog, Holmes, refuses to bark.
My dad's truck, which we call
the "Green Death," refuses to start
and I cannot go outside.

I've been thinking about a question
I want to ask you:

"What's the most beautiful thing
you know about horses?"

The reason I'm asking

is that I'm a stranger to horses
and horses are strangers to me.

Let me tell you why.

I am half Indian and I am half white.
The good news about all this is
I could be the cowboy *or* the Indian
when we used to play Guns.
The bad news is my family never had
any horses to ride up here.

All's we had up here were dogs.

My Mom is a Dogrib Indian.

Our people have great respect for dogs.
Dogs used to help us haul camp
and protect the food stashes when we
would hunt for caribou out on the barrenlands.

My grandfather, Pierre Wah-shee,
used to sneak into wolf dens
to gather wolf cubs
so he could breed them with dogs.
This way, his dog team who were
half wolf and half dog would be *deadly!*

We are not horse people.

If I could, I'd shake hooves with all the horse tribes.
My granny taught me that handshakes
are hugs for strangers.

If I could speak to horses

I would ask them a few questions:

Do horses have secrets?

In winter, do they wonder,
"What do the leaves do under the snow all day?"

Do horses think fireworks are
strange flowers blooming in the sky?

Do horses think the northern lights
are a heaven for horses—or a shower of love
from the Creator to all of us?

Do horses love?

In Dogrib, we say

tłı (tlee) for "dog."
Our word for horse is *tłıcho* (tlee-cho)—
which means "big dog."

When did dogs grow into horses?
When did horses shrink into dogs?
Do horses call dogs "little cousins"?

When horses and dogs talk to each other,
what do you think they say?

When they dream of each other,
what do you think they see?

Let's do some investigating.

Let's ask people: "What's the most beautiful thing
you know about horses?"

Let's ask my dad, my mom,
my crazy brothers, Johnny and Jamie.
Let's ask my buddy Mike
because my brother Roger is in Costa Rica.
Let's ask my friend Heather and my friend George.

Let's ask everyone I talk to today,
on January's coldest day of the year
in my hometown of Fort Smith
in the Northwest Territories:
"What's the most beautiful thing
you know about horses?"

What do you say, partners?

While Dogrib Indians say, "Ho!"
Cowboys say, "Let's go! Let's go!"

My dad is chopping wood.

I ask him: "What's the most beautiful thing
you know about horses?"

"The most beautiful thing about horses," he says,
"is they always know their way home."

"Wow," I say.
Maybe our dog, Holmes, is part horse.
She always finds her way back home
after she breaks her chain and runs to play
with her friends down the street.

What is Holmes doing outside on a day so cold
the snow is holding its breath?
Being teased by ravens, that's what.

My mom is making
cinnamon apple pies.
"Mom," I ask, "what's the most beautiful
thing you know about horses?"

"Horses?" she smiles
as she runs her hands over the dough.
"They must have secrets.
When they run they seem to flow over the land.
Sometimes I think they like
to compete with the wind.

"They also have very beautiful eyes."

I ask my brother Johnny
who's looking at himself in the mirror:
"What's the most beautiful thing
you know about horses?"

"Their hair," he says. "It's super cool."

Ha-ha! Johnny locks himself
in the bathroom for hours and hours
just so he can comb his hair to perfection.
He combs and combs and combs it free.

If he were a horse, he'd have
the most beautiful mane.
It would shiver and ignite as he ran
with his brothers:
Roger, Jamie, and me!

I ask my brother Jamie

who always lets the fire go out in our woodstove
because he's too busy watching
the World Wrestling Federation:
"Jamie, what's the most beautiful thing
you know about horses?"

"They can run sideways," he says.
"What?" I say. "They can't run sideways. Can they?"
"Watch them sometime," he says
and goes back to watching WWF wrestling.

I look behind us. Sure enough,
the fire has gone out. No wonder I am freezing!

Where did Jamie get to see horses run sideways?
I think of the dogs up and down our street.
Holmes can't run sideways.
Snowball can't run sideways.
Bullet can't run sideways.
Can they?

I would like to ask my brother Roger
what's the most beautiful thing
he knows about horses,
but he's in Costa Rica on vacation.
Maybe he's riding a horse and thinking of me.

So I'll ask my buddy Mike in Roger's place:
"What's the most beautiful thing
you know about horses?"
"I don't like horses," Mike says.
"Why?" I ask.
"Because you feel great all day when you ride them
but after that you feel bowlegged."

I guess that's a good thing
about having dogs instead of horses.
I've never felt bowlegged in my entire life!

Thanks, Holmes!

I call my friend Heather

in Yellowknife and ask her:
"What's the most beautiful thing
you know about horses?"

Right away she says,
"My favorite horse is the Appaloosa
because an Appaloosa is a horse with freckles."

I smile and think of my mom.
I used to be shy when my freckles came out
in the summertime
until the day my mom told me that
every freckle is a little kiss from God!

Are Appaloosas shy
behind their freckles too?

I talk to my
friend George Littlechild.

George is Cree. His people are horse people—
just like my people are dog people.
When I close my eyes and think of him
I see a blue horse running free.

"George," I say, "what's the most beautiful thing
you know about horses?"

"Their breath," he answers. "I love their breath.
You can feel their breath move through their chest.
They stare at you as they breathe.
Their soul comes right out."

The Cree word for horse is *mista'tim* (mis-ta-im).
It means "big dog"—just like *tłıcho* (tlee-cho)
in the Dogrib language.
Isn't it neat how both our languages
call horses "big dogs"?

Now that we've found out
all these beautiful things about horses,
what could we find out about
all the animals of the earth if we called
everybody in the whole world?

Here are some of the secrets I learned
the last time it was this cold.

I learned that an eagle
has three shadows.

I learned that frogs
are the keepers of rain.

I learned that there's an animal on this earth
who knows your secret name.

Well, partners,

puppies need lots of sleep and so do I.

But before I go for my nap,

let me ask you:

"What's the most beautiful thing

you know about horses?"

"And what's the most beautiful thing

you know about you?"

When my publisher, Harriet Rohmer, asked me to write a book about horses, I was the first to admit that horses were strangers to me. You see, I am a member of the Dogrib Nation from the Northwest Territories in Canada. We are not horse people. It is much too cold up here for horses—but I've always been curious about them. It was my curiosity that inspired me as I wrote this book. By asking my family, my friends, and my collaborator and friend George Littlechild their thoughts on horses, I learned some odd and sweet things about what my people call the tłıcho (big dogs). And I also learned more about my family and friends. I found my curiosity was very contagious and soon I had the whole town talking and wondering about horses.

I made a promise to myself to ride my first horse before this book came out. On my summer holidays, I had the honor of riding Fran, a bay mare, in Keremeos, British Columbia. I don't think I've ever felt anything so beautiful in my whole life as riding a horse. The trust between a horse and rider was unlike anything I've ever felt before. The only thing I can compare it to is the trust George Littlechild and I shared as we worked together to share our story with you. I hope you enjoy our book as much as we enjoyed creating it.

Mahsi Cho! Thank you very much! —RICHARD VAN CAMP

Richard Van Camp is a member of the Dogrib nation from the Northwest Territories of Canada. An emerging voice in the contemporary Native American literary movement, he was named "the most promising author under 30" by the Canadian Authors Association. His first children's book, *A Man Called Raven* was well-received in the United States and Canada.

George Littlechild is an internationally-renowned artist from the Plains Cree nation. He has created two widely-acclaimed books for Children's Book Press, *A Man Called Raven* and *This Land Is My Land,* which won the prestigious Jane Addams Picture Book Award and the National Parenting Publications Gold Medal. Littlechild lives in Vancouver, British Columbia.

Editor: Harriet Rohmer
Design and Production: Lucy Nielsen
Editorial/Production Assistant: Laura Atkins

George Littlechild would like to thank Adam Sundown. Thanks to David Schecter for his editorial help. And thanks also to the staff of Children's Book Press: Sharon Bliss, Shannon Keating, Janet Levin, Emily Romero, Stephanie Sloan, and Christina Tarango.

Children's Book Press is a nonprofit publisher of multicultural literature for children, supported in part by grants from the California Arts Council. Write us for a complimentary catalog:
Children's Book Press, 246 First Street, Suite 101, San Francisco, CA 94105.

Distributed to the book trade by Publishers Group West.

Library of Congress Cataloging-in-Publication Data
Van Camp, Richard
What's the most beautiful thing you know about horses? / story by Richard Van Camp ;
pictures by George Littlechild.   p.   cm.
Summary: On January's coldest day of the year in a small community in the Northwest Territories,
a stranger to horses searches among family and friends for answers to an important question.
ISBN 0-89239-154-5   [1. Horses—Fiction. 2. Northwest Territories—Fiction. 3. Métis—Fiction.
4. Indians of North America—Canada—Fiction. 5. Questions and answers—Fiction.]
I. Littlechild, George, ill. II. Title.   PZ7.V26247Wh 1998   [E]—dc21 97-37437 CIP AC

Printed in Hong Kong through Marwin Productions.
10   9   8   7   6   5   4   3   2   1